The Little Vessel

ISBN 978-1-64140-485-3 (paperback)
ISBN 978-1-64299-537-4 (hardcover)
ISBN 978-1-64140-486-0 (digital)

Christian Faith Publishing, Inc.
832 Park Avenue
Meadville, PA 16335
www.christianfaithpublishing.com

Printed in the United States of America

The Little Vessel

LeighAnne Clifton

One day, the Artist crafted a small vessel. He had made many other vessels: delicate vases with intricate detail, large platters with exquisite painting, and sturdy pitchers. As was the case with each of the others, this vessel was very special to Him. After making her, He set her on a shelf to dry so the Artist could later use her. While she sat there, some of the completed vessels began to talk about the new little vessel as if she weren't there.

"She's very plain, isn't she?" asked the beautiful, delicate vase.

"Yes, and quite small too," agreed the large, lovely platter.

"What purpose do you think the Artist could ever have for her?" the sturdy pitcher asked his friends. "She's just a plain tiny bowl."

As she listened to their comments, the little vessel began to believe that maybe she didn't have a purpose, that she indeed was useless. She loved the Artist very much, but maybe He was wrong to make her as He did. Maybe she should have been bigger or more ornate.

"Pay no attention to them," said a voice from another shelf. It belonged to a dainty teacup.

"But maybe I *don't* have a purpose," the little vessel complained.

"Of course, you do," answered the teacup knowingly.

"How can you be so sure?" she asked. The little vessel was so confused, not knowing whom to believe.

"Little vessel," the teacup explained with patience, "my friends and I have belonged to the Artist for a long, long time. We've watched Him create many wonderful things."

As he said this, the little vessel noticed for the first time that the teacup was not alone. There were other teacups, all similar to her new friend but none of them exactly alike. And behind them sat a rather nondescript little teapot. None were particularly beautiful, some were chipped with worn paint, but all looked very comfortable on the Artist's shelf.

"So what is *your* purpose?" the little vessel inquired of any of the teacups that might choose to answer.

Each one smiled kindly, but the teacup that had addressed her before replied, "Little one, every day the Artist selects several of us to serve Him. What an honor it is to be chosen by Him! However, those of us who are not used that day are content to wait patiently, knowing He will use us in His time."

"And that's it? You just sit there waiting?" the vessel asked, not quite able to believe the response. It seemed a dull existence, and yet all the teacups continued to smile in contentment.

"Oh, no," countered the teacup. "Sometimes we're used for special occasions. Or perhaps one of us will be used to take milk to a needy neighbor. And when the Artist has visitors, He'll use all of us at once! Some of us have even been used to hold beautiful blossoms from the Artist's magnificent garden."

The little vessel had so many more questions. How would she find her purpose? What would happen to her if she indeed didn't have one? What if she didn't like what the Artist had planned for her? But all her questions would have to wait because at that moment the Artist came and took the little vessel off the shelf.

13

He gently placed her in the kiln and turned it on. Soon the little vessel was subjected to extreme heat. At one point, she cried out, "Please, make this stop! I can't take this anymore! I don't want a purpose if this is what it takes!"

Eventually, the temperature began to drop, and the little vessel cooled. The Artist came back and removed her from the kiln.

He carefully and lovingly examined her shiny new finish. The little vessel basked in her Creator's admiring gaze.

How lovely I must be now, she thought triumphantly. *He seems so pleased! Surely now I'll find out why I was created.* With these happy thoughts, the little vessel was once again placed among the other vessels to await her turn to be used.

As she waited, she heard the finished vessels talking among themselves.

"Do you see that?" the pitcher whispered.

"Yes," answered the vase. "What a shame. She could have been quite pretty and useful."

"Well, I suppose the Artist will discard her now," guessed the platter.

The little vessel could stand it no longer. She had to know what they were talking about. What could be wrong? The Artist had looked at her so approvingly.

"What are you talking about?" the little vessel demanded. "What is wrong with me?"

"You have tiny little holes all around your edge. You're supposed to be a vessel, but you can't hold much water. It can happen when you go through the heat of the kiln. I'm sorry, but the Artist won't be able to use you now."

The little vessel was devastated. She desperately wished she were attractive like the platter, or tall and delicate like the vase, or sturdy like the pitcher, or useful like the teacups.

But I'm none of those things, she thought with a broken heart. *I'm flawed, and now the Artist will never be able to use me.*

"Cheer up, little vessel," consoled the teacup. "The Artist has plans for you."

But the little vessel just sat there quietly, feeling very sad and sorry for herself. Soon, the Artist returned to the place where all the vessels were waiting. He immediately reached for the little vessel. She felt certain that He was going to throw her out, broken and unwanted. But how wrong she was!

The Artist took the little vessel, several other bowls, and various pieces of pipes. And He set to work. It wasn't long before the little vessel sat atop a stunning fountain in the middle of a lush, beautiful garden. The Artist addressed the fountain.

"I've wanted a fountain for this spot in the garden for a long time. I created the little vessel especially to sit atop this fountain. You see, little vessel, while you were being formed I placed tiny holes in you. Now, as you are filled, you'll overflow in all directions, filling not only the bowls below you but also watering the beautiful flowers all around you."

So the little vessel spends her days joyfully being filled with water and overflowing into the Artist's fountain and garden. Occasionally, she will see her friends during a lovely tea party, and they will smile at each other. The Little Vessel has finally found her true purpose.

Deeper Thought Study Questions

1. (a) Where in the Bible do you see the artistic, creative attributes of God? (b) How are they displayed? (Genesis 1, Nehemiah 9:6, Psalm 139:14, others)

2. (a) What is wrong with comparing ourselves to others? (b) Did God create everyone with the same purpose? Why? (1 Corinthians 12)

3. (a) When we go through trials and difficult times, does it mean that God has abandoned us? (b) On the other side of your trial, can God use you and the pain you have endured? (John 16:33, Romans 5:3, James 1:2–3)

4. The teacup in the story was a steady source of encouragement for the Little Vessel, even when the others were discouraging. What are some ways that you can be an encouragement to people around you who may need to hear that they are loved?

5. Proverbs 3:5 tells us, "Trust in the Lord with all your heart and do not lean on your own understanding." (a) Did the Little Vessel do that at first? (b) Do you find it difficult sometimes to trust in the Lord with all your heart?

The next verse comes with a promise: "In all your ways acknowledge Him and He will make your path straight" (Prov. 3:6). When we acknowledge God's sovereignty over our lives, things aren't easy, but they glorify Him. What are some ways you can acknowledge Him in your day-to-day life?

6. The Little Vessel had been created to allow water to flow through her. Often in the Bible, we see Jesus referred to as Living Water. (a) Can you find some of these references to Jesus? (b) Why is it important to think of Him as Water?

7. The Little Vessel poured water not only into the fountain and but also into the surrounding garden. If we think of the fountain as fellow Christians and the garden as those who don't know Christ, how can your calling as a Christian line up with the Little Vessel's? (Acts 1:8).

8. We see that the Little Vessel would stay put for the time being. Sometimes the teacups would travel to the needy. (a) Does God call everyone to go far away for a long time to serve Him? (b) In what ways can you serve Him close to home?

About the Author

LeighAnne Clifton lives in Aiken, South Carolina, with her husband Bill and their cats. They met at the University of South Carolina while earning their chemical engineering degrees. They have two grown children, a son and a daughter, both teachers. She works as an environmental engineer and enjoys teaching Sunday school. LeighAnne enjoys Bible study, painting, gardening, and upcycling furniture. The Little Vessel is her first published work.

CPSIA information can be obtained
at www.ICGtesting.com
Printed in the USA
BVHW021636120120
569254BV00003B/12/P